rabbit ears

First published in Great Britain in 2006 by Bloomsbury Publishing Plc,
36 Soho Square, London, W1D 3QY
This paperback edition first published in 2007
Text copyright © Amber Stewart 2006
Illustrations copyright © Laura Rankin 2006
The moral rights of the author and illustrator have been asserted

Typeset in Cheltenham Light
The art was created with acrylic inks and paints on Arches watercolour paper
Design by Filomena Tuosto

A CIP catalogue record of this book is available from the British Library

ISBN 9780747589662

Printed in China by South China Printing Co
10 9 8 7 6 5 4 3 2 1

All papers used by Bloomsbury Publishing are natural, recyclable products made from
wood grown in well-managed forests. The manufacturing processes conform to the environmental
regulations of the country of origin.

rabbit ears

Amber Stewart

illustrated by Laura Rankin

BLOOMSBURY
CHILDREN'S
BOOKS

To my very lovely Lottie and Josh
I love you—clean ears or not
—A.S.

For Tyler and Ryan
—L.R.

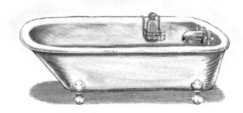

Hopscotch knew what he liked, and what he did not like.

He did like Rabbity,

building a tower
twelve blocks high
with no wobbles at all,

and very chocolaty chocolate cake
(with extra icing on the side).

Hopscotch did not like
lumpy pudding,

cold wet paws,

and losing Rabbity just before bedtime, even though Rabbity
was usually found exactly where Hopscotch had left him.

And Hopscotch knew, for absolute certain,
the thing he did not like the most was . . .

...having his ears washed!

Hopscotch liked his ears dry. He didn't like them soapy.
The soap always ran away then ended up in his nose
and made him sneeze. The sneezes shook him from his
soggy, drippy ears to his toes.
Hopscotch didn't like it one little bit.

Hopscotch would do a lot not
to have his ears washed.
With Rabbity's help,
he would hide them.

Sometimes he'd pretend that
he had suddenly turned into
a cat – a cat with very small,
clean ears.

Or he would hold on to them very, very tightly.

Hopscotch's mummy tried tricking him...
"Where's the airplane?"

Hopscotch's mummy tried begging him...
"Please, just this once?"

She even tried chocolate cake . . .
"Look, it's your favourite."
But nothing worked.

One day, Hopscotch's big cousin Bobtail
came to stay – just for one day and a night.

Hopscotch and Bobtail played high jump, long jump.

Then they listened for danger as they rescued Rabbity from the lion's den.

They played and played until all too soon it was suppertime.

"When can I go and stay all by myself at Bobtail's?" asked Hopscotch through a mouthful of extra-chocolaty chocolate cake.

"When you are big, little Hopscotch," said Daddy. "When you are big." After supper, it was time for a bath.

Hopscotch was happily playing submarines
when he noticed something odd...

Bobtail was washing his own ears!
He didn't seem to mind the runaway soap.
Not one bit.
And he didn't get the sneezes at all.
Not one sneeze.

Big rabbits wash their own ears, thought Hopscotch.

Hopscotch felt it might be a good idea
to practise ear-washing on Rabbity first.
Rabbity didn't seem to mind it at all –
in fact, they had fun with all the bubbles.

"What are you up to, Hopscotch?" asked Daddy.

"I'm practising," said Hopscotch.

"Practising what?" asked Daddy.

"Practising washing my ears so I can be big and go and stay with Bobtail all by myself," said Hopscotch.

"Well," said Daddy, "that's wonderful!"

Hopscotch knew what he liked and what he *really* liked.
He liked bathtime with Rabbity and clean soapy ears.

He *really* liked singing a song with Mummy
to celebrate his very clean ears.

Soapy, soapy, soapy ears, soapy ears,
* soapy ears.*
Washy, washy, washy ears, washy ears,
* washy ears.*
Fluffy, fluffy, fluffy ears, fluffy ears,
* fluffy ears.*
All day long!

And, best of all, he liked
packing his favourite games,

waving good-bye to Mummy and Daddy,

and going to stay with big cousin Bobtail for one
whole day and a night all by himself. Well, almost...

. . . Rabbity came too.